# Marshmallow M

# Marshmallow Magic

## By: Gail Gilla Czyszczon

## Edited By: Izabella Czyszczon

Layout and Design by Louie Romares

ISBN: 979-8-7183-4083-9

# Marshmallow Magic
## The Biggest Order Ever

Empathy is their magic ingredient.

Follow candy-crazy Mila and her besties, Maia and Maci, as they run Marshmallow Magic—perhaps the best cake and marshmallow pop business on earth!

From their dream-come-true backyard tree fort bakery, can the girls stay positive as they face challenges with their biggest pop order ever and save Mrs. Bradley's reading event?

The trio of girl bosses unite to navigate tricky pop shop snafus as well as third-grade social dilemmas and—along the way—discover a creative idea to inspire countless readers across their Midwest neighborhood.

Each of the books in the Smart Senses series deals with challenging issues like food allergies and dyslexia so that kids know they aren't alone when they feel left out.

This feel-good story on friendship, resilience, and sweet treats is a hit among kids and parents alike.

# Other Books In this Series

Book 1 – Marshmallow Magic: The Biggest Order Ever – Released March 23, 2021

Book 2 – Marshmallow Magic: Saving Spring Soccer – Coming Summer 2021

Book 3 – Marshmallow Magic – Coming Winter 2021

# CHAPTER 1

G otta admit it.

It was my best idea yet.

A new dessert design.

Honestly? It technically was a whole new treat category.

"Presenting the world's first triple-layered marshmallow cake pop!" I cheered.

Maia eyed the sweet treat I'd sketched in the school playground dirt. "Love the layers, Mila, but that gooey worm wiggling around the sprinkles is gonna chase any customers away."

We both burst out laughing at the sight and fell over in the grass. We'd been doodling since the recess bell had rung, quite sprinkled ourselves in dusty dirt. Together with our other bestie, Maci, we run Marshmallow Magic—perhaps the best marshmallow and cake pop business on earth! And it *is* the most magical part of our third-grade lives.

We make pops that look like everything from narwhals to soccer balls using some **concoction** of candy, sprinkles and melted chocolates. We deliver them to birthday parties, sports celebrations, and feel-good fundraisers throughout our neighborhood, Westmont.

- *concoction: a mixture of various ingredients*
- *You try: My friend and I used a concoction of_____ and _____to make _____.*

Westmont is, like, the happiest place ever. People are always celebrating something. Babies born. Games won. Animals helped. You name it, someone's happy about it. If you were looking down from the moon, I imagine that Westmont would shine from the collective glow of birthday candles and camera flashes capturing moments to remember.

"Now that school's back, I hope we get pop orders for class parties," Maia said. Her neat, shoulder-length hair barely budging despite the rest of her twirling with excitement. Her daily, signature barrette that she wore on the left side of her hair was purple today to match her purple and denim outfit. Maia was always calm, cool and coordinated. Her style was simple, but somehow sophisticated. Her perfect posture seemed to match her always-on confidence, and I liked that about her. Whenever I felt a little nervous, just knowing I had a friend like her made me feel calm and cool, too.

"Ooh, remember each third-grade class earns a party when they read a total of a hundred books together?" I said, fluffing my extra-thin, blonde ponytail. I have to use extra small hair ties or else I'd be winding the regular ones around my hair forever. At least I was one of the tallest girls in third grade, so that kind of made up for my barely-there hair. "Between Maci and Brighton, I bet Mrs. Nelson's class is already halfway there!"

We both glanced over and saw our friend Brighton in his typical reading nook under the big birch tree. Maci and Brighton were well known as bookworms. Maci always had a new novel tucked under her arm, waiting to steal a moment to nose-dive back into the story.

"Well, I'm one hundred percent getting s'mores marshmallow pops when our class hits a hundred books!" I said.

Making pops with Maia and Maci is for sure my happy place. Can I tell you something? I'm allergic to nuts, fish, and eggs. So I have to be super careful not to eat them. Sometimes they're hiding in foods you'd never expect. Like, did you know nuts are often in bread? And that eggs can be in ice cream or pudding? Super sneaky, I know.

Can't lie: I sometimes feel left out when I can't eat treats at a party or playdate. And when I go to restaurants with my family, some of the best things *on* the menu are *off*-limits to me. My heart skips a beat every time I hear the ice cream truck but bursts when my parents check the wrapper label and find peanuts on the list. Total buzzkill for my would-have-been brain freeze!

But I have a secret strategy for staying smiley. It all started when I noticed something. Something really interesting. I realized that I can either see the food I *can't* eat or the food I *can* eat. They're side by side in the fridge. Same goes with anything, really. I can see the good things or look around and see sad stuff too. It's all right there. All the time. The big, glorious universe of everything!

OK, ready for this? So, when I'm getting sad, I pretend I'm wearing special glasses. I close my eyes and imagine putting on glasses that allow me to focus clearly on only the positive things.

I even call them my Positive Peepers! I've gotten really good at knowing when I should put them on. My stomach starts to feel woozy, and my face tightens up. I keep thinking about what I don't like over and over. Basically, my body goes bonkers.

### Smart Senses

*OK. Being school smart is important. Sure, we all know that. But did you know what else is super-duper important? How you feel! If you can understand how you and others feel, you're going to have a way better life. That doesn't mean you'll always be happy. Being sad, scared, or mad are totally normal. It's how you choose to act that matters.*

*I learned an awesome trick called Smart Senses to help. These are a bunch of cool ways to tune in to how you're feeling so you can decide what to do. Ready?*

*Here are my first two:*

- *Smart Sense #1: Positive Peepers – Fake glasses that help you focus on the positive things in life, even though sad stuff is there too.*
- *You try: Can you think of a time some-*

*thing sad happened but you saw the*
*good side?*

- *Smart Sense #2: Body Bonkers – When*
  *your body goes crazy before you realize*
  *you're worried about something. Like*
  *a woozy tummy, a headache, or jittery*
  *thoughts that keep coming like a water-*
  *fall.*
- *You try: What are some crazy things*
  *your body does when you're worried?*

The Peepers work like magic. The things that aren't so great are always there, but they get blurry while I focus on happy things. I'm already bummed that I can't have some foods, but it would be way, way worse if I let that spoil my day.

So, while life has thrown me some challenges, it's kind of OK.

Gotta admit it: being able to bake, dip, frost, sprinkle, and taste test any way I want totally makes me feel free! Add my two besties in that mix, and that's the best recipe ever.

\*\*\*

"Remember the beach ball–shaped cake pop order?" Maia

asked.

"It was so tricky to get three colors on one pop!" I replied. "They turned out so amazing. The birthday girl flipped out when she saw them. You were smart to let each color dry before we dipped the next color," I said.

Maia laughed. "It was eighty-five degrees outside and a melted rainbow mess inside our kitchen."

"I miss summer already!" I said in sudden realization that it was fall. We lived just outside of Chicago, Illinois, in the midwestern part of the country. The leaves were just starting to change bright red and orange, and the air was finally starting to cool off a bit.

Maia suddenly looked serious. "Mila, we haven't had an order in three months. If Marshmallow Magic is going to stay alive, we need to get down to business!"

I nodded in agreement. She was right. We needed to find Maci and make a pop plan pronto!

As we re-created the beach ball pops on the dusty ground, a familiar red soccer ball rolled across our canvas, wiping out our summer scene.

"Maci!" we shouted in unison.

# CHAPTER 2

**M**aia and I sprung up from the ground to **intercept** Maci's ball before she could. As she raced in our direction, I passed the ball to Maia and ran toward the two matching oak trees to position myself for a shot on our makeshift goal. I stood in the grass, ready to score, when Maci sole-rolled Starry—her nickname for her beloved ball covered in glossy white stars—from Maia and darted off in the opposite direction like the champ she is.

- *intercept: to stop something or keep something from happening*
- *You try: I intercepted my dad at the front door before he could see the _____ I had made for his birthday.*

"Starry, you're my hero!" Maci said, laughing while she flipped her long, wavy brown hair over her right shoulder. Maci is the most girlie sports star I know. She always has a dazzling cluster of ribbon decorating her long ponytail. Somehow the glitter, beads, and ribbon bounce along with her through a full day of soccer, school, and tree climbing. She wouldn't have it any other way.

She also has more than two dozen pairs of soccer socks. And I'm not talking plain, boring soccer socks. All of them are full of color, design, and sparkle. Her mermaid socks with sequin scales may be her favorite, but hands down, the giraffe ones with the long ribbon tongues are the best.

I can't decide if her passion for fashion seems surprising since she's so sporty, or if it makes perfect sense. Maci's intense about everything she does, and I love that about her. She always says, "Gotta work hard but play harder!"

Maci is shorter than me, but she's way stronger. Honestly, her muscles look flexed even when she's chilling out. One time she was eating a popsicle at a park with me when a football flew at her head. She caught it with her non-popsicle hand without even blinking and threw it back at the quarterback. She's outside playing sports all the time, so sometimes I'm not sure if her skin is tan from the sun or naturally from her Brazilian family.

Maci's been one of the Westmont Bears' midfielders since she joined this spring. A couple years before that, she was the star striker (scorer) of the recreational soccer games that her dad coached.

*** 

I was craving a snack, so when Maci was busy adjusting her ribbons, I quickly stole the ball from her and kicked it toward the playground benches.

"My pretzels and cheese stick are calling me!" I said, with my friends chasing me.

We all snagged our bags and plopped down on the weathered wood benches.

Maia peeked inside her bag. "Granola bar and cherries. Yes!"

"Score!" said Maci with a fist pump in the air. "Animal cookies and banana."

Maci found an owl-shaped cookie and made it fly over to Maia and carefully land on her shoulder. "This wise owl wants to help you with your math homework!" Maia played into the imaginary scene and cuddled up with the cookie before eating it.

Maci then exclaimed, "No way! Mila, you won't believe it. I found an endangered flamingo in the zoo box! I've never found one that wasn't broken! It's a miracle." She excitedly grabbed the frosted flamingo, made it walk across the bench, and placed it on my napkin with dramatic effect.

As much as I wanted to giggle, I suddenly felt my face tense up because I knew I couldn't eat the cookie that now seemed to be staring at me.

Body Bonkers began.

Couldn't find my Positive Peepers anywhere.

I'd seen that brand of cookies at Fresh Market, and my mom said I may be allergic to them. I tried to hide my sadness through a half smile, because Maci is always trying to make me laugh.

Ignoring my flamingo, I tried to hold back tears and focus on my snack. I tried *not* to think about *not* being able to eat another treat, so I started stacking my pretzels up by size. Biggest on the bottom for a base, smallest on the top. "Focus, Mila," I told myself.

Maci and Maia exchanged glances. They noticed that I

got quiet and wasn't my bubbly self. It was obvious that I didn't gobble up the flamingo like Maia did to her owl. Good friends are, well, good at knowing when something is making you sad.

"Oh, Mila, I'm so sorry!" Maci suddenly exclaimed with her worried face. "I didn't even think about whether the cookie had nuts. I was so excited I found an unbroken flamingo for you."

She checked the label and read aloud with a sigh, "May contain traces of peanuts."

### What Is a Food Allergy?

*A food allergy is when my body thinks a food is bad. If I eat it, my body tries to keep me safe by tightening my blood vessels. My face, mouth, and chest also could get itchy and rashy. My throat could swell, making it harder for me to breathe, which is why it's really important I stay away from these foods. I wish I could just tell my body, "Hey, a peanut butter cup is a good thing." But that's nature for you. And I can't change it.*

"I'm fine," I heard myself say, even though I wasn't fine. Even though this happened before like a gazillion times, it never seemed to get easier. It's not like one frosted flamingo would

change my life, but I hated feeling left out. Even among my two best friends. I was having Body Bonkers and my tummy continued to feel woozy and I just wanted snack time to be over.

Maci and Maia simultaneously hugged me with a tight squeeze. They clearly were having an Empathy Alert and were so sweet to care. "Mila, I think it just may be Marshmallow Magic time after school!"

Finally able to breathe without almost crying, I started to feel better and managed to squeak out, "Cool."

- *Smart Sense #3: Empathy Alert – When you use clues to figure out how someone is feeling.*

"Tree fort at two fifty-five?" Maia asked.

"Yep!" Maci and I said at the same time.

Sometimes I don't even need to pull out my Positive Peepers when I have my positive peeps—Maia and Maci. And just like that, I was back to feeling good.

# CHAPTER 3

There I sat in my third grade classroom, staring at the clock. 2:47, 2:48, 2:49. Ugh. Still 2:49.

*Rrrring!*

The 2:50 school bell! Finally, it was time to head to the tree fort.

Our class headed out the door, down the hall and outside toward the parking lot curb where parents waited for their kids. My mom was there in her straw Bermuda hat and some colorful shirt, always under the second tree where the shade is best. Her personality is about as colorful as her wardrobe, and she was always finding ways to infuse magic into our family. Like the time she served breakfast for dinner (like, I'm talking pancakes *with* chocolate chips and whipped cream) or the time she surprised us with a set of one hundred paints and mini canvases after school.

I ran up to her. "Mom, I'm going to run ahead home to the tree fort, okaaaay?" I said as I continued right past her.

"Hi...and bye, Mila!" my mom said, smiling, and launched into a light jog to keep up.

We only live a block away, and Principal York stands at the corner to help kids cross every day.

I finally reached the tree fort after racing home from school. The sight of Maci's and Maia's backpacks at the foot of the oak tree meant they were already up there in what I consider a magic tree fort bakery. It's where we operate Marshmallow Magic. Then I glanced up to the top of the fort and saw it. The pop order signal! This is a green light that Maia put in that comes on whenever an order comes in through our website.

She somehow wrote computer code to make the green light turn on when we had a new order in our email inbox. Something like:

[IF MAILBOX = +1 NEW EMAIL, THEN TURN SWITCH ON]

There were physical wires that connected the green light to the computer, so some type of electrical magic shot through the wire. I swear I felt the electricity in my veins, too, every time I saw that green light. And we really needed a pop order. Goodbye, lazy summer days; hello, awesome autumn action!

*Double yay!* I thought to myself as the combination of that green light and my friends meant super sweet good stuff was about to happen.

I added my doughnut-design backpack to the pile and climbed up the crooked wood ladder on the tree trunk. I flung open the tree fort door, taking a moment to admire our logo, as I always do. Maci was submerged in a beanbag chair with her nose deep in a book about mythical dragons. I could only see her thick, brown eyebrows over the book, but they revealed her every emotion. Like now they were arched super high, which meant she was at a surprising part of her book. She didn't notice me come in, but Maia paused from ticking away at her computer keyboard and looked at me more excited than I'd ever seen her before.

"Milaaaa!" she sang with her arms in the air. "You won't believe it: we just got the biggest order ever in the history of Marshmallow Magic!"

My day just kept getting better. Green light pop signal on. Backpacks at the bottom of the tree. Biggest order ever? I had to **verify** what Maia had said.

- *verify: to make sure*
- *You try: I had to verify that my parents said I could*

  *_____, because they normally say it's too*

  *dangerous.*

"Wait, bigger than the four-dozen pop order for the animal shelter fundraiser last spring?" I inquired.

"Bigger," Maia said, collecting herself and smoothing down her hair, which had become wildly disheveled upon announcing the order.

"Six dozen?" I guessed.

"Bigger." Maia widened her smile with each number.

"One hundred?" I said.

"Double!"

"Two hundred?" I gasped. "That's insane! Really?"

"It just came in while we were at school from Devin Bradley's mom," Maia explained. "You know, the one who volunteers in the library and runs the Reading Adventures program around the holidays. Her email said that she's now running her reading program in other parts of the city this fall and wants to kick off each location with a fun event. She wants marshmallow pops at the registration tables to attract the kids."

"Banana split! This is the best order ever!" I said ecstatically, jumping up and down with Maia.

Maci still sat silent, engrossed in her dragon book.

Maia and I eyed each other, amused. "Maci!" we both hollered. "Are you alive?"

Maci turned her head toward us slightly, her big brown eyes still glued to the pages before her.

"Two hundred pops, Maci!" we shouted.

"Huh?" Maci's attention slowly diverted to us. "Two hundred what?"

"We get to make two hundred pops for the biggest order ever for Devin Bradley's mom's reading program next weekend!" I explained to her.

Suddenly Maci rolled out of the beanbag chair, sprawling out on the floor. "Wow. Wait, wow!" she exclaimed. Maci then quickly had a change in expression from excited to concerned and said, "Wait, that's a *lot* of pops. How will we ever get that many done? I have soccer practice two days next week, plus the agility clinic at Spreckels Park Thursday."

Maci twirled a lock of her hair repeatedly on her forefinger while her thoughts began a similar **unruly** spiral: "I can't miss practice, but I know you need my help on this order. We can't let our biggest customer ever down. Word would get out that we can't handle big orders, and then we'll never grow our business!"

- *unruly: wild, disorderly*
- *You try: Our new puppy was so unruly as he _____in our living room.*

Maci was having a Wild Worry attack!

- *Smart Sense #4: Wild Worry – When you can't stop worrying about something and think about all the bad things that could happen.*
- *You try: What are the top three things you worry about?*

# CHAPTER 4

Maci spun around the tree fort, grasping for a solution. The sound of a basketball bouncing caught her attention. She peered out the window and saw Parker T. from my class shooting hoops in his driveway. He lived next door and had always been pretty cool—for a boy.

Parker was about my height but seemed taller because he was so good at basketball. His sandy brown hair was swept off to one side when it wasn't in his eyes. He was mostly shy unless you knew him well. I thought he was friendly and kinda goofy—well I guess when he wasn't being shy.

Maci said, "I need to shoot a few baskets." Maia and I watched her disappear down the tree fort pole, off to burn some nervous energy. Sports always helped her mind calm down.

Moving briskly, Maci hopped over the fence, startling Parker, and his basketball bounced wildly into a bush.

"Oh, hi, Maci," Parker said. "What's up?"

"Mind if I shoot a couple? I need to move a little to stop worrying," Maci replied.

"Sure, no prob—but you're gonna have to get past me," Parker said, bounce passing her the orange rubber ball and getting into defensive position.

"You're on!" Maci said, catching the ball and taking off down the driveway toward the basket.

As they played, Parker shared with her, "I've had a pretty stressful day, too. B-ball is my go-to."

"Yeah, we got the biggest pop order ever, and of course I have the busiest week ever. I don't know how we'll get it done," Maci said, taking a three-point shot. The ball swooshed in the net, and Parker did his best shocked look.

Smiling, Maci asked, "So what's up with you?"

"Aw, my parents are making me stay after school to get help reading, but it's kinda embarrassing to have people in class see me." Parker looked deflated.

"Totally get it," Maci said. "Well, maybe you could borrow some of my books or something. I have like a million."

"Thanks, Maci, but I don't think I could get through those huge chapter books you read," Parker said. "I think I have to go in for dinner now. Later." With that, Parker walked into his house and shut the door.

Maci sighed, unsure if she was feeling better or worse.

***

She hopped the fence and climbed the tree fort ladder. As soon as her face emerged up the hole inside the fort, Maia and I knew she still was worried.

Maia came to Maci's rescue with reason, as usual.

"Maci, today's Friday. If we want two hundred pops ready by next Friday, that's eight days and they stay fresh for weeks in the fridge. Two hundred pops divided by eight is twenty-five. Even if only two of us work together for the next eight nights, we can totally do twenty-five pops a night, right? Or we could even do fifty pops on four days," Maia said calmly, cycling through matching pens in three shades of blue in her peacock-themed notebook that she brings everywhere to think.

<u>Pop Schedule Option One</u>

Friday – 25 pops

Saturday – 25 pops

Sunday – 25 pops

Monday – 25 pops

Tuesday – 25 pops

Wednesday – 25 pops

Thursday – 25 pops

Friday – 25 pops

TOTAL – 200 pops

Pop Schedule Option Two

Friday

Saturday

Sunday

Monday – 50 pops

Tuesday – 50 pops

Wednesday – 50 pops

Thursday – 50 pops

Friday

TOTAL – 200 pops

Maci straightened her sequined socks, stood up, and grabbed a strawberry soda from our minifridge. To signify her change in mood, she let out a breath, flipped her hair, made her silly scrunch face, and said, "My brakes were busted again. *Seeing the numbers always fixes my Brain Brakes.*"

- *Smart Sense #5: Brain Brakes – Something you do that stops you from worrying. Playing sports or seeing facts helps Maci calm down. What helps you calm down?*

It's true. Maci is a worrier. Ever since I've known her, she's been so focused on doing a great job, whether she's taking a test or scoring a soccer goal. She wants to please people and achieve great things, which is good.

But when messing up makes her feel **inferior**, we've gotta help her. She's amazing just as she is, whether she scores a goal or gets a good grade. Once she starts to worry, her thoughts tend to keep going as if her brain has broken brakes.

- *inferior: worse than something else*
- *You try: The _____my brother made were inferior to the ones my mom makes.*

Maia is fabulous at reasoning with her, which helps Maci *see* a solution. We sometimes call her "the Mechanic" because it's like she works on Maci's car brakes with a wrench. She tightens them up and—poof!—Maci is back to her positive self.

"Numbers know," Maia said, satisfied with her work.

We all smiled and plopped down in the beanbag chairs in **unison**.

- *unison: at the same time*
- *You try: On Christmas morning, me and my little brother ran down the stairs in unison to _____.*

"Maci, read the order!" I said, riding on a wave of excitement.

"OK!" Maci read the email from our tree fort computer. "So, it arrived at 2:03 p.m. today."

- Name: Briana Bradley
- Phone Number: (919) 555-1234
- Email: bbradley@email.com
- Event: Four Reading Adventures kickoff events at libraries in the community

- Event Date: Saturday, September 10
- Marshmallow or Cake Pops: Marshmallow
- Total Quantity: 200
- Theme: Reading, books, wise owls, cheerful colors—you choose

My mind instantly flooded with design ideas. Book-shaped pops with gummy "bookworms" popping out. Owls with cocoa cereal flakes for feathers. Chocolate chip owl ears and Skittles eyes. Periwinkle, purple, and jade-colored owls with matching pop sticks. I was just itching to start doodling. Just the thought of a blank slate for two hundred pops would keep my mind occupied for days to come.

I've always been more artistic than athletic. I think of my fashion as a paint canvas and think I have kind of a combo artsy-glam look going on that's all my own. Well, I admit I try to dress like the pop singer Gloria—my absolute idol. I play piano and want to be as good as her someday. During one TV performance, she wore this blue sequined shirt with super soft and fuzzy leggings as she sang "I Am Me" from behind a white baby grand piano. It's my favorite song and I have an outfit that kinda looks like the one she wore, only they're pajamas.

Uncomfortable pajamas.

There's also a drawer in my desk with notebooks full of dessert drawings and sketches of the bakery I'd love to own someday. All my schoolwork has pop design ideas in the margins. Give me a pencil, and ideas just start flowing. There are truly infinite ways to put together cake, candy, and marshmallows.

But we had to stick to our schedule for Mrs. Bradley's order. We all had busy weekends, so we decided to go with schedule two.

We needed to begin first thing after school Monday if we were going to deliver this order on time and keep Marshmallow Magic in business.

# CHAPTER 5

The 2:50 school bell.

That happy sound.

The signal I wait for every day.

Not that I don't skip to school every morning—it's just that when I hear that noise, I know it means tree fort time! After a fun family-filled weekend, it was Monday, and I couldn't wait until school ended to get dipping our first 50 pops for Mrs. Bradley's order.

So, there I sat in Room 3 at 2:30 at table cluster number three, tapping my number two pencil, staring at the clock. My teacher, Mrs. Driscoll, was in a particularly good mood today. During reading groups, she updated our progress charts with some brand-new glitter stickers shaped like various gemstones.

I was hoping for an amethyst but ended up with an emerald. I think they're technically rarer, so it was OK.

I love the new book series we've been reading on historical inventors like Thomas Edison and George Washington Carver. Did you know Thomas Edison didn't really invent the light bulb? After ten thousand tries, he *refined* the incandescent light bulb to make it easier for all homes to have them. Whoa. I repeat: whoa!

I admire him for not giving up after ten thousand tries! He must have had some seriously powerful Positive Peepers. I for sure would have struggled to invent even a hundredth version of anything!

Well, maybe if it were marshmallow pops, I can see that. I could invent like a thousand, no problemo. OK, so maybe Edison just loooooved light bulbs like I love pops!

After I finished answering the questions on the worksheet Mrs. Driscoll handed out, I studied the book sticker chart. Our class had read thirty-seven books altogether. Most kids had read two books, but Parker T. hadn't read any. Zero gemstone stickers. I noticed him sitting on the floor with the rest of his reading circle, hugging his legs. He was staring out the window with glassy eyes. I wondered if something was wrong. He looked sad to me, but I didn't know why.

*Rrrring!*

The happy sound!

I grabbed my backpack and jumped in line in the second spot, right behind Keira A. My last name comes right after hers in alphabetical order, so she is like the forever line leader. I'm only first when she's sick, which has only happened once so far. I'm happy she's not sick, though, because she's so nice. She once picked up all my crayons—even the ones that rolled under Ryan C.'s icky basketball shoes—when my pencil case dropped off my desk. Plus, I love checking out all her backpack charms while I wait for Mrs. Driscoll to round up the rest of our class.

I think Keira and I are kind of class leaders in addition to being the line leaders. I like school, and the rules make it fun, like a game. Line up, get out your pencil, draw a picture, solve a problem…it's like one long day of games to me.

Finally, Zachary W. took his place at the end of the line, and we started to shuffle out the door, down the hall, and outside toward the parking lot curb.

My mom was there again. Yep: same straw Bermuda hat and colorful shirt under the second tree. I basically flew past her.

"Tree fort," I informed her.

"Hi...and bye, Mila!" my mom said.

I waved to Principal York as I dashed across Acorn Lane, down the secret path behind the houses, across Pine Cone Drive (my street), over the side fence, and into the backyard.

Everyone has a **sprawling** backyard in the Midwest. The grass is thick and soft and one of the truest greens I could imagine. My dad keeps sweet-smelling flowers, fruit trees, and poufy plants everywhere. Huge purple hydrangea bushes line the fence. A sturdy apple tree stands at command in the center of the yard, ready for a determined climber to snatch a snack any time of day. Bright green and dark purple leafy bushes weave between an assortment of flowers.

- *sprawling: spread out over a large area*
- *You try: My sprawling _____ were on my messy bedroom floor.*

I darted down the grass and bounded over the minibridge, past the birdbath to the far back corner where the great oak stood towering over our property like a guard. It seemed to be unshakable, even in the worst Chicagoland storms. Sometimes when I hear a noise at night when I'm in my bed, I'm comforted by the great oak being there. Something about knowing there's something consistent, sturdy, and sure so close to home makes me trust that everything will be OK.

***

When Marshmallow Magic orders started spiking the summer before we started second grade, Maci, Maia, and I totally took over my kitchen. We had multiple orders every week. We had marshmallows, cake mix, dirty bowls, candy, spoons, and mis-dipped messes on every surface in our kitchen. When Mom kept finding sprinkles in the silverware drawer, we knew she'd had enough.

She told us we had to find a new place to run our pop business.

Our garage had way too many spiderwebs. Maci's pool house smelled way too much like chlorine. Maia's attic seemed hopeful, but after our first order of pops melted into a mess, we had to brainstorm other options.

We needed a place that had enough room for our supplies and our imagination as we handcrafted every order.

A place that had electricity to plug in our candy melting machine, as well as running water to clean up our supplies.

A safe, dependable place that we could make our own.

Then a light bulb went on in my head! Kind of my Thomas Edison moment. The great oak!

# CHAPTER 6

The great oak was the perfect place for Marshmallow Magic pop making. After our collective squeal quieted down from the **notion** of a tree fort bakery, Maci, Maia, and I started drafting out blueprints for our dream.

- *notion: idea*
- *You try: I didn't like the notion of getting up at _____ a.m.*

We took our vision seriously and spent days making lists of materials we'd need to build the tree fort, as well as sketches of how it would be built into the tree.

Maia put our ideas into a high-tech slideshow, including information about how we would use part of our money from our business to pay for the project.

Our parents approved our plans in like a split second. Guess they must have liked our presentation.

That summer, I learned to use a hammer, saw, measuring tape, and level (which makes sure boards aren't crooked even though they look straight). All of our parents took turns helping us nail in boards to make a ladder up the main trunk, secure in a base floor, put up the walls, position holes for windows, and nail in a weatherproof roof.

Mrs. Nguyen—one of our customers who raves about us to her friends—donated a bunch of wood. There were twenty-four boards, and we needed to space them out every two feet around our rectangle fort. Maia loves numbers like I love candy. She loves them even more when they're in the real world and not in a math workbook.

"Ready for real-world math, guys?" Maia asked, bursting into a happy dance. "We need enough long boards to fit around the **perimeter** of our fort. We need one board every two feet. OK; so we first need to measure the sides of the fort."

- *perimeter: all the sides of a shape added up*

Rectangle fort

Two long sides – 12 feet each

Two short sides – 10 feet each

Total perimeter = (12 x 2) + (10 x 2) = 44 feet

"OK, stand by! I am computing!" Maia went into deep thought, then finally exclaimed, "We need to divide forty-four feet by two to see how many boards we need. That's twenty-two!" Maia said with her head buried in her notebook, scribbling numbers and lines systematically down the page.

I jumped in to confirm we had enough wood. "Cool, we have twenty-four boards, so that's two more than we need."

"Right!" Maia exclaimed. "Mila, you've got this perimeter thing down."

"Seriously, you make math fun. It just looks like a bunch of numbers to me until you make it come alive," I said in response.

Maia is drawn to math and technology like I am to art, music, and cooking.

If her brain looks like a computer circuit board inside, mine is like a paint palette. Together, it's like electric wires in a colored pattern!

After the frame of the tree fort was done, we insulated the walls, installed the windows, added drywall, and connected the electricity to our main house. When things got complicated, my dad invited his carpenter friend over for dinner to ask a few questions.

Finally, in August, it was time to paint the walls and bring in some furniture. We all agreed to go with a light-blue-and-white theme to mirror Marshmallow Magic's brand. We even painted our logo on the door.

Maci's mom helped us put up some shelves for storing supplies.

We added a worktable, three beanbag chairs, a small desk, and a whiteboard for brainstorming.

We strung some LED lights all over and framed some of our original pop design sketches to hang on the walls. I filled glass mason jars with all sorts of candy from Candy City, my favorite candy store, which sells hundreds of types of colorful candy from bins. You can take as much or as little of any candy they have. It's all the same price, so sometimes I'll make a master mix in my bag and eat three special candies each day after dinner. Some days it's chocolate graham, gummy worm, and then rock candy. The next day it might be Red Vines, taffy, and then caramel.

When the tree fort bakery was finally done, Maci, Maia,

and I and our families all stood in my backyard. I remember it so clearly. The sun had just set, and the clouds in the sky looked like rainbow sherbet. We all stood on the cool grass, silent, just gazing at the fort, thinking about all the memories that were about to be made.

Maia suddenly looked as though she had an exclamation point appear over her head like in the cartoons and said, "Wait! It's not done yet! We forgot the finishing touches!"

Maci and I looked at each other and knew she was entering her mastermind mode. We came up with this term because she seriously transforms into someone else in some kind of brilliant turbo mode. Once, she rearranged her bedroom from a sweet, stuffed-animal-filled haven to a Halloween haunted house overnight. Different electric buttons and wires would make all sorts of things happen, like stuffed bats flying across her ceiling with spooky sounds and flashing lights.

So, we cleared the tree fort and let her have the stage. The technology she added that summer took our fort to a whole new level.

# CHAPTER 7

*B*ack to the present

I made it to the tree fort and it was time pop-dipping time. I saw Maci's and Maia's backpacks at the foot of the oak tree, added mine on the pile, and raced up the trunk. All three of us squealed as I burst through the door. Every order kicked off with a squeal. It wasn't like we tried to make this a tradition. The squeal just happened. Like a secret language. Every time.

Maia got right to work. She sat upright at the computer desk with her narrow shoulders at full attention and her fresh, powder-white face aglow from the monitor screen.

Her glitter pens were ordered from left to right in ascending shades of blue: crystal aqua on the left, sky blue and periwinkle in the middle, with shades like cobalt and stormy blue on the end.

Sticky notes in various sizes and colors were stacked up neatly in a basket, ready to display short reminders to buy chocolate chips or unplug the candy melter.

A matching stapler, hole punch, and tape dispenser decorated with gemstones were positioned within arm's reach off to the right.

Her workstation **invigorated** her and was her place for productivity.

- *invigorate: to make full of energy and excitement*
- *You try: Invigorated by the warm air, I went to the park and _____.*

After a few cheerful squeaks and pen strokes, Maia had timelines ready for everyone on pale-blue marbled paper and handed them out proudly with a flick of her wrist. I always was amazed at the big ideas that would come from her tiny, delicate hands.

"Big Bradley Order" was printed in sophisticated cobalt-blue lettering at the top of the page, with—as always—a very detailed plan of action.

### Monday

3:30 p.m. – Brainstorm pop ideas

3:45 p.m. – Call customer to confirm order

3:50 p.m. – Check supplies and make shopping list

4:03 p.m. – Get ride to Candy City to buy supplies

4:45 p.m. – Test pop designs

5:05 p.m. – Make 50 pops


**Tuesday** – Make 50 pops

**Wednesday** – Make 50 pops

**Thursday** – Make 50 pops

**Friday** – Wrap pops and put in boxes

### Saturday

8:00 a.m. – Meet at tree fort to deliver pops by 9:00 a.m.

I always feel confident and calm when Maia takes charge. She loves making lists, organizing plans, and finding ways to make things work. I think Marshmallow Magic would just be a bunch of chaotic sprinkles without her. I mostly like designing pops and baking! Maci is the horsepower behind getting all of the work done. She makes pops at twice the rate that I can. I guess we three friends go together like sugar, flour, and eggs. Best mix in history.

I took my typical station at the side of the whiteboard and loaded up my pockets with dry-erase markers, ready for a team brainstorm.

I wrote "Big Bradley Order" at the top of the whiteboard in blue and said, "OK, what did Mrs. Bradley say she wanted for the theme?"

"Owls were a part of their brand," Maia said.

"Reading is the theme," Maci added.

I wrote down:

Owls

Reading

Books

Wisdom

Cheerful colors

"OK, so we could maybe make the pops shaped like owls or books. What other things go along with these?" I asked.

"What about trees for the owls, glasses for reading, bookworms, alphabet letters, school..." Maia brainstormed.

"Great ideas!" I said, scribbling more words on the whiteboard.

"What colors do you think would be good?" Maci asked.

"When I think of owls, I think of brown, maroon, and tan, but I guess those are a little dreary. Maybe we could do something like bright orange, persimmon red, lemon yellow, and shimmery gold," I suggested.

"Oooh, so cute-iful!" Maia said, using her word for something cute and beautiful.

The colors just came to me and started swirling around into images in my head. I sketched out my vision on the whiteboard. I first drew a marshmallow, then transformed it into a bright-yellow owl with large orange ears and red wings.

"We can use triangle candy corn for the ears!" Maci exclaimed.

"And red licorice for the wings!" Maia chimed in.

"Loooove it!" I said, super satisfied with our first design. "We should have at least three designs to make the order more interesting. What if we made colorful red and orange marshmallow pops and added alphabet letters on them?"

"Sure," Maci said.

When I finished drawing the design options, Maia announced, "It's 3:35 p.m., and we are officially ahead of schedule."

Everyone was in a great mood now.

"OK, everyone vote for their top three pop designs, and then let's call back Mrs. Bradley to confirm her order!" Maia said, whisking Maci's attention back to business.

Maia handed us all three colored sticky notes to use to cast our votes. We all jotted our favorite designs down and tossed them into a basket. Maia read them out loud, and we ended up with the yellow owl. For the alphabet pops, we chose an orange pop with white coconut flakes on the top and a red pop dipped in white nonpareils, which are like tiny sprinkle spheres.

I was in love with the designs, but the customers didn't always love what we loved. One time we made ninja pops for a boy but it wasn't the right kind of ninja. He cried right there at his own birthday party, and we vowed to always show a sample to customers first after that.

It was time to call Mrs. Bradley. We had zero time left to come up with new ideas. Would she like the designs as much as we did?

# CHAPTER 8

Maci and Maia huddled near me as I picked up the telephone that was designed to look like a piece of cake with pink frosting roses and strawberries. The plastic phone worked on old technology. It was connected to the wall with a long, curly wire that stretched across the whole tree fort if you—for example—had to go check if there were enough purple candy melts midcall.

3:38 p.m.

I dialed the phone number. *Brrrring. Brrrring.* "Hello?" said Mrs. Bradley.

"Hi, Mrs. Bradley. This is Mila from Marshmallow Magic. We got your order and have three design ideas," I explained proudly.

"Hi, Mila! That's wonderful. I was hoping I didn't put in

my request too late. We're excited for our Reading Adventures rollout and wanted it to be extra special."

"Well, we're happy you did! We'll deliver your two hundred pops to the four libraries by nine a.m. Saturday, September tenth. We have three pop designs, including a yellow owl and orange and red pops with alphabet letters. I emailed you a picture of the drawings we made, and we hope you like them!" I told her.

"One more thing: our pops are dairy- and nut-free for anyone with those food allergies. We do use ingredients like coconut and food dye, which some people are allergic to. We post a sign and include a copy of all of our food labels in case customers ask," I explained.

"Wow! I'm so impressed with how detailed your team is!" Mrs. Bradley said.

"Thanks so much! We'll get to work!" I said, closing out the call.

Maci and Maia were jumping up and down, basically doing gymnastics and silently cheering through the whole call. I had to keep spinning away from them to avoid laughing, the long telephone cord now wrapped around me like a tornado.

We all eyed each other in our minihuddle and instinctively burst out "Banana split!" at the same time, chiming together about our most exciting Marshmallow Magic moment yet.

3:43 p.m.

"We're ahead of schedule by seven minutes too! Time to list the supplies," Maia announced, pen perched in her hand while she grabbed her clipboard.

We went through all the typical supplies at the top first to make sure we had enough.

Marshmallows – Have 100, buy 100

Candy melts – Have 5 bags, buy 5 bags

Food dye – Have enough

Coconut oil – Buy 1 jar

Pop sticks – Have enough

Pop wrappers and twist ties – Have enough

Delivery boxes – Have enough

"OK, now on to the candy decorations we need," I said.

"We need candy corn for the owl ears, red licorice for the wings, and chocolate chips for eyes. For the alphabet pops, let's make sure we have coconut and white nonpareils. What should we make the alphabet letters out of?" I asked.

"Maybe we can use those fancy candy letters you see on birthday cakes," Maci suggested.

"But those cost like twenty-five cents a letter!" Maia said. "That would cost too much."

"Isn't there a breakfast cereal with alphabet letters?" I asked.

"Yes! Great idea," Maia said.

"I guess we could try that, but we've never used cereal on our pops. What if they crumble or don't stick well?" Maci looked worried.

"I think we have to try new things. How about we ask Marcos and Maria to be our taste testers?" I asked, referring to Maci's older brother and younger sister.

"No-brainer—they'll have candy any day, any time," Maci said.

3:56 p.m.

The final shopping list included:

> *Candy corn*
>
> *Red licorice*
>
> *Alphabet cereal*
>
> *Coconut*

*White nonpareils*

*Marshmallows*

*Candy melts*

"It's 3:57 p.m., and we're still ahead of schedule! Let's grab our money and ask your mom to drive us to Candy City, Mila," Maia said.

Maia unlocked our bank box with the silver key she carried around her neck at all times. She grabbed our Marshmallow Magic wallet and put it safely in the top zippered pocket of her backpack. We all lined up and—one by one—slid down our tree fort pole, landing in the soft grass below.

Per our tradition, we each chanted "Charge!" on our way down, as if we were some sort of fearless baking warriors. We skipped toward my house to find my mom. I flung open the back door and yelled, "Mooooom!"

There was no answer in the house, which suddenly seemed way too **desolate**. Maia and Mila joined in the search and shouted, "Mrs. C!"

- *desolate: empty and quiet; no signs of life*
- *You try: The playground seemed desolate because*

*the weather was so _____.*

Finally, my dad peeked his head out of his office. He had his headset on as well as a fancy collared shirt on top, but plaid pajama pant and old slippers on the bottom since people only saw his top half during video meetings. He did his best goofy-Dad dance to highlight his frumpy outfit and said in a half-silly, half-annoyed voice, "Shhhh! Sorry, Mila. On a work call. Your mom took Tommy and Ana to swim lessons and will be back in about an hour." Then, he pretended to be air swimming like my siblings and disappeared behind his office door again, leaving us in complete silence.

I seriously could hear Maci gulp.

My stomach started to tighten.

Even Maia looked slightly shaken.

How were we going to get the supplies in time without a ride to the store? We'd planned our schedule so tightly and didn't have room for delay if we were going to get this order done on time.

Unless we got to Candy City pronto, Marshmallow Magic's reputation could turn sour forever.

# CHAPTER 9

"OK, everyone, breathe," I ordered, trying to get a grip on the situation. "Option one: wait until my mom gets home and work later at night."

"But don't you think your mom is going to make dinner when she gets back?" Maci asked.

"And my dad would kill me if I stay up past my bedtime. Not an option!" Maia declared firmly.

"OK, option two: we could start working with the supplies we have until tomorrow when we can get to the store," I brainstormed desperately.

"We can't do any of the pop styles without the new supplies, though. The candy melts will harden, and we need to put on the candy decor right away." Maci started to twirl her hair with despair.

I felt out of options. My stomach was in a full-blown pretzel knot. Wild Worry thoughts were starting to flood my brain. Body Bonkers were kicking in for sure.

I had felt like this before.

Many times.

I knew what I had to do.

I had to put on my Positive Peepers.

Without anyone knowing.

So, I closed my eyes and put them on. I started to focus on the positive things:

1. We'd been through lots of hard times with Marshmallow Magic before. We always figured out some way to fix things.
2. We had our biggest order ever, which meant customers liked us. We must be doing something right.
3. Candy City wasn't that far away.
4. My friends were hard workers, and we still had lots of time left.

I could feel it.

An airy, calm feeling that slowly filled my brain. My stomach was getting stronger.

I had it—the idea that would save our biggest order ever!

"I've got it! Candy City is about two miles away, so we could ride bikes if Mei or Jun could ride with us. They're both home on Mondays, and we could offer to give them sample pops to thank them," I **serenely** said, satisfied with what my Positive Peepers had discovered in a previously bleak situation.

- *serenely: calmly*
- *You try: After studying all weekend for the spelling test, I serenely_____.*

"You're right—they're home and do love our pops! That just may work, Mila," Maia said. Mei and Jun are her older (and, I think, ultracool) twelve- and fourteen-year-old sisters. "Let's go to my house. Mila, get your bike!"

We bolted out my back door to grab my bike from my garage, then headed over to Maia's house three blocks away on Birdbath Lane. Maci led the way, running even faster than I was pedaling, and Maia jogged behind, somehow scribbling in her trusted notebook as she hobbled down the sidewalk. "4:02 p.m.! We're almost behind schedule!" she announced. Maci and I just giggled, fueled with optimism. Nothing was stopping this order now.

When we got to Maia's, we went inside, and her sisters were both sprawled out on the couch. Mei had arranged all the couch pillows into a nest and was wearing printed leggings and a baggy sweatshirt, accessorized perfectly with her high-top basketball shoes. Jun was sunk deep into the space where the pillows used to be and was wearing a shirt that read, "Kind Is Cool," with cutoff jeans that were dyed bright pink. They were laughing about some story we just caught the end of.

"So, I told her, 'That emoji seriously confused everyone, and they thought you were crying about Ryan, not laughing!'" Mei said, tossing another pretzel stick in her mouth.

"Hey, Mei and Jun! Wondering if one of you may be able to bike with us to Candy City in exchange for some pops! We just got our biggest order yet but can't find a ride," Maia said.

"You should go, Jun. I have basketball practice. Plus, you can bike past Ryyyyan's house, and maybe he'll be outside mowing the laaaawn," Mei said to her older sister, who apparently was now officially boy crazy.

"Um, sure. Not a bad idea. I could use some fresh air after six hours at school anyway," Jun said.

Maci, Maia, and I all whispered "Banana split!" and low-fived behind our backs.

We headed off to Candy City, almost like we were on the yellow brick road to Emerald City in the play *The Wizard of Oz* that our school put on last year. This pop order adventure was just beginning.

# CHAPTER 10

C andy City is every kid's favorite store. It's like a life-size Candy Land game board.

The entrance was made to look like rainbow-colored licorice twisted into an arch. The oversize Candy City sign glowed in bright neon colors. At night, it lit up the whole block with bright pink, green, and orange light while illuminating the faces of sugar-seeking patrons as they entered the store.

There were hundreds of peek-through bins filled to the brim with candies like gumdrops, caramels, meltaways, jelly beans, and gummy bears. Workers wore old-fashioned ruffled orange aprons with the Candy City logo on them, and their pockets were always full of individually wrapped hard candies to surprise shoppers with.

Popular music hummed from hidden speakers, keeping an upbeat mood jamming throughout every corner of the shop. Dozens of kids raced through the store at any given time, closely followed by slightly agitated parents. The most exciting part of the store was a full-size slide where kids could whisk down into pretend oversize marshmallows.

It was like a dream. Like, an I-want-my-birthday-party-here dream.

You actually can host parties there, but that's a topic for another time.

As much as I love to browse the bins for the better part of an hour every time I visit, we had to get our supplies and go, go, go!

We split up to save time, and Maci and Maia tossed red licorice and white nonpareils in my basket as I hunted for candy corn. I found the seasonal aisle and was getting a little sidetracked by the beach ball–shaped gumball collection. I didn't see any candy corn and started to scurry left and right, checking every bin to make sure I didn't miss them. Suddenly it occurred to me that most of the candies were summer themed. I raced to find a worker and spotted one kneeling down in front of the sprinkles section, aligning containers neatly on the bottom row.

"Excuse me, where can I find candy corn? I checked the seasonal aisle but—" I said.

"Oh, those should be in the first week of October," he said before I could finish my sentence.

My heart began to race. We'd already told Mrs. Bradley that we would use candy corn for the owl ears. Candy corn was the perfect shape, color, and size for the ears. Nothing else would do!

There I stood, frozen in the sprinkles section of Candy City, unsure what we could do without candy corn. Just then, Maci tossed icing writers and crystalline sugar into the basket, just like basketball free throws, and Maia followed shortly with a bag of coconut.

"We can grab the alphabet cereal at Fresh Market on the way home," Maci said, slowly noticing my solemn mood.

"Wait, what's that look?" Maia asked.

"Candy corn is a fall item and won't be here for three weeks! They were perfect for the owl ears, and I can't think of any other candy that would work," I said, without a hint of hope in my voice. I didn't even want to try out my Positive Peepers at this point. It had been hard enough getting to the store, and we still had so much to do.

"Mila, don't give up now!" Maci said. "You're always the one who keeps me positive, so we can figure this out. How about we try to find something else in the store that may work?"

"You're right. We have to try," I said reluctantly.

"OK, everyone report back to aisle five in five minutes with any options for candy owl ears!" Maci declared and raced off through the store as if it were a soccer field.

In exactly five minutes, we all met. I had hoped Maci and Maia found something better than the square orange Starbursts I brought that we could cut in half to make triangles. I suspected they were too heavy and would slide down the pop before it dried.

Maci brought rounded orange gumdrops, but an owl's signature feature is its pointed ears.

Maia found some coated candies that were shaped like small squares. She argued that we could press half into the marshmallow to create a triangle shape. I thought these were the most hopeful, but we had to buy a huge bag of assorted colors where only like 25 percent were orange or yellow.

"Banana splat," I said sadly, quite the opposite of our happy "banana split" celebration catchphrase.

Suddenly Maci and Maia burst out laughing. I guess it was kind of funny, but you-have-to-look-really-hard-for-it kind of funny. There we were with three second-choice owl ear options and backup supplies for alphabet letters—busted business owners who needed to make some magic happen. Ginormous banana splat if you ask me.

The burst of laughter fueled my spirit just enough to check out at the cashier and pedal home.

Ya know, sometimes my Positive Peepers are my positive peeps—my best friends! When I'm feeling pessimistic and can't think of good solutions, my friends swoop in and keep me positive. We're like a seesaw sometimes. When one of us is up, the other may be down. So, my friends lift me up. But a seesaw isn't quite right. Because when one of them lifts me up, we all stay up! Maybe we're more like soda pop. When one bubble goes up, all the others follow to create an unstoppable **effervescence**!

- *effervescence: bubbles in a liquid; enthusiasm*
- *You try: Do you have friends that make you laugh or help you stay positive like effervescence?*

"OMG! It's 4:55 p.m. We are seriously behind schedule!" Maia exclaimed. "We need to get back to the fort to test the pops before dark!"

# CHAPTER 11

After checking out at Candy City, we biked down Main Street, turned right on Oak Grove Parkway and left on Pine Cone Drive, and turned into my driveway, lined with purple hydrangea bushes. We thanked Jun and quickly darted back to the fort and loaded up the tree's basket with our new supplies.

The basket is connected to a pulley so we can lift up heavy supplies from the top of the fort. After my dad got concerned when Maci was scaling the ladder with two large bags and lost her balance, genius Maia designed the basket system out of things she found in her garage.

When Maia showed up with a slideshow and a tiny demo version of a tree, basket, and **pulley system** in a shoebox, my dad's face lit up like the Candy City sign.

- *pulley system: a rope attached between a wheel and something heavy, so when the wheel turns, the object is pulled to a new place*

Maia installed the life-size version of the pulley basket with her parents' help. It was working within an hour, and we never had to strain our backs again on the ladder.

So, up went the three random non–candy corn candies and other supplies. They clocked in at 6.7 pounds altogether. (Oh, did I forget to mention that Maia had wired the basket to register weight on a digital display at the top of the pulley so we could monitor strain on the system? She thought of everything.)

In sharp contrast to the sophisticated pulley system, we all climbed the wobbly ladder boards up twelve feet to the fort, where it was finally time to get pop making!

Maci and I laid out all the supplies on the center table while Maia wrote the order on the board. I clicked on some music, which streamed through the overhead speakers. The LED lights pulsed to the beat. Maia had hooked up the music to the lights so they blinked in rhythm to the songs.

"Can we test the owl design first?" Maci asked.

"For sure—can't wait!" Maia and I chimed in.

We set up the melting machine and poured candy melts inside. We added food coloring and a little bit of coconut oil for shine. Meanwhile, we set out the red licorice for the wings, chocolate chips for the eyes, and the three hopeful options for the ears. Next, we stuck a few pop sticks in marshmallows and lined them up for dipping.

Once the candy melts were smooth and warm, we stirred in the food coloring evenly and dipped the first pop. We set it in the pop holder, and Maia put on the wings and eyes.

Slowly and gently, I put the orange halved Starbursts on top of the marshmallow for the ears. We held our collective breath. The Starbursts seemed to stay put for, oh, maybe half a second until they came sliding down the sides of the pop, plopping on the table.

"Ugh," we all let out as we accepted that this option was not going to work for the ears.

"Let's try the gumdrops," Maci said, offering up ear option two.

She put two yellow gumdrops on the owl pop with careful

precision. We all looked at the pop. The gumdrops were perfectly fixed on top. But something wasn't right. We all started to smirk at the strange sight that now looked more like a confuzzled (confused and puzzled at the same time) mouse than a wise owl.

"OK, the gumdrops are a no go, but a yes go for taste testing!" I exclaimed.

I shoved the whole pop in my mouth before we could vote on who the taste tester should be. Candy is my favorite indulgence—I even have a stash of secret candy in my bottom desk drawer. Pretty sure my parents know but don't say anything. In fact, sometimes I find surprises like new markers or minty gum in the drawer. And let me tell you: it's not the treat fairy. Thanks, Mom and Dad!

Having food allergies means missing out on some treats and snacks. And by "some," I mean, like, a lot. At parties, playdates, restaurants, school events, grocery store sample booths, on airplanes—everywhere. So having a little snack attack makes me feel a bit more in control. Which, hey, I guess I really am. I can eat *lots* of treats.

Anyhow, Maci and Maia just got fake mad when I ate the pop, then laughed a second later. We all knew we got to eat the mess-up pops. Kind of the best part of Marshmallow Magic!

"OK, last option," said Maia. "Time to try the hard-coated candies." She dipped another pop and carefully placed two orange square candies on top, pushing half of them into the marshmallow to expose just half the squares to make triangles.

We all watched as the color from the candies started to bleed into the candy melt. It began looking like orange-yellow lava with streams of murky color dripping down the sides.

"Bummer!" Maia said as she chomped the whole pop in one bite, making her feel slightly better.

Then there was silence.

We all knew this was the last option, and it was a flop. The fort was so quiet that the other background noises seemed louder. The soft swooshing of the tree leaves blowing in the wind. The **sporadic** sound of kids playing in the neighborhood. The angry thumping of Parker's basketball. The distant sound of a train miles away. Then, the sharp chirp of a blue jay.

- *sporadic: every now and then*
- *You try: My sporadic attendance at basketball practice meant that _____.*

I found myself getting lost in the bird's song.

It was a happy melody that made the rest of the world melt away. It calmed me down.

Suddenly, I noticed that the blue jay was sitting on one of the tree fort windows!

"Look!" I said excitedly, pointing at the bird. "It's not even afraid of us."

"Wow!" Maci said. "What's in its beak?"

The bird had a burlap bag in its beak. It was cinched closed with a bright-yellow ribbon. I slowly approached, and it stayed on the windowsill, studying me with friendly eyes.

The bird then dropped the bag on the counter below.

Stunned, I walked over and opened it up.

"Girls...you will never, ever, ever believe what's inside," I said with a rush of magic running through my body.

# CHAPTER 12

Maci, Maia, and I peered inside the burlap bag. Nestled inside was a collection of shiny orange-and-yellow candy!

"It's candy corn!" we all cheered. "But how, what, why…" I was at a loss for words as to how this bird could bring us a bag with the single most important ingredient we were missing. Nowhere in Westmont—perhaps the world—was candy corn for sale yet.

"I'm so confuzzled," I said.

It was as if this miracle blue jay had flown from a faraway candy galaxy to save our order.

We looked over, and the blue jay continued chirping. It fluttered its wings and flew off into the sky. We raced over, but

as soon as we looked out the window, it was gone as fast as it had appeared. Just like that. Poof.

"Hmm...if there really is magic in Marshmallow Magic, this is it!" I told Maci and Maia.

After we all slowly awoke from a state of awe, we knew we had work to do. And now. There was no time to wonder about the blue jay or whether we were in some type of fairy tale.

We flipped the candy melter back on, lined up marshmallows on sticks, and added the candy corn to the mix of **embellishments** on the table where they awaited their fate atop a pop.

- *embellishment: decoration*
- *You try: I wanted my _____ for my grandma to be extra special, so I glued on embellishments before I put it in the envelope.*

After repeating the dipping process, we tried out the new ears. Presto! They stayed perched on top as if the wise ol' owl pop knew all along this was the best solution.

We added the wings and eyes, then proudly placed the

first owl in our tiered pop stand, which neatly displays three dozen pops like a piece of fancy artwork.

Steadily, we worked together to fill up forty-nine more of the pop stand spots with nearly identical pops.

6:05 p.m.

We sat back with delight, admiring fifty little owl faces that minutes before had been blank white canvases. We were one amazing team of confectioners. We had the perfect combination of artistic ideas, hard work, and organization. Together, we made great things happen.

But sometimes past our dinner curfew.

"Ack!" Maia exclaimed. "We're late for dinner! Girls, great work, but we gotta gooooo…" she continued as she slid down the tree fort pole.

Maci gave me a puppy-dog-eyes look as if to ask for permission to leave without cleaning up. I gave her a nod, and she disappeared into the darkness down the pole.

Exhausted and hungry, I turned off the candy melter, put the dishes in the sink, wiped the table, and clicked off the lights. "Good night—oops, I mean, good morning—owls," I whispered to the treats lined up in the pop stand, respecting real owls'

**nocturnal** nature.

- *nocturnal: awake during the night, asleep during the day*
- *You try: I really think my teenage brother is nocturnal because he_____.*

It was dusk, and just a glimmer of light remained in the sky. In the silence, I looked over to Parker's empty driveway. A few leaves fell from the tree in his yard, and I noticed Parker sitting up in the branches, snapping off twigs. His house glowed with warm light, as if begging him to join his family inside. But he seemed immovable there on the second branch from the bottom. I was going to call out to him, but I had to listen to my stomach pleading with me for food.

My attention shifted to the faint scent of dinner coming from my house. I was glad I wasn't the only one who had spent the evening working in a kitchen. I slid down the pole and headed into my house for some of my dad's homemade Polish **pierogi**.

- *pierogi: a Polish food similar to a dumpling filled with cheese, potatoes, or other fillings*

My dad's parents grew up in huge families in the southern part of Poland. And by huge, I mean like ten brothers and sisters. My grandma's family—Babcia, as we call her—grew up on a farm. All the kids slept in one big attic together. I can't even imagine being in the same room with my six-year-old twin brother and sister for too long, let alone sleeping in the same room every night. I guess times were different then and you just went with the flow and couldn't imagine anything better.

Babcia beams whenever she tells stories from Poland, so clearly her heart was as full as their house. All the kids had some role on the farm. Some dug up potatoes, others fed the chickens, and others helped sell things at the local market. My babcia helped mostly at the market and hand painted signs for the foods and treats their family sold. She had a creative energy and was always coming up with cool ideas. She plays the guitar, and sometimes we catch her playing Polish music in the garage, painting some piece of furniture or canvas.

Dziadzia's family (that's my grandpa, or my dad's dad) grew up in a similar setting on a farm. But in addition to the farm, they also ran a bakery in the heart of their medium-sized village. They grew things like sugar, berries, and wheat and made cream and cheese from the milk of the farm animals. They created delicious pastries, breads, and cakes. Never too sweet. Everything in Poland seems to brim with delicate flavor, which, surprisingly, makes it even better than super sweet treats. He regularly bakes his favorites for our family. The kolacky cookies are the best in my third-grade American girl opinion.

My dad still tells me stories about the bakery, and I swear I feel like I've been there. It was small but packed every day with Polish patrons, friendly conversation, and fresh-baked treats in every window.

But tonight—tonight is pierogi night. I took my usual seat at the dinner table across from Ana and Thomas, my twin siblings. They were already fidgeting and appeared to be having some kind of ball-kicking contest, not all that well hidden under the table. I giggled under my breath—half-amused, half-annoyed. My mom was putting the finishing touches on the table. She put out glasses of milk and napkins and lit a candle. My dad proudly emerged from the kitchen dancing with a plate full of steaming pierogi. They can be filled with farmer's cheese, sauerkraut (cabbage), blueberries, and more. My favorite were the cheese ones. I basically stole two before the serving platter hit the table.

"Someone's hungry!" my dad said, smiling. "Wait! I forgot the best part!"

"The topping!" Ana cheered. She was right. No pierogi was complete without the special sour cream sugar topping.

I filled the rumbling space in my belly while my heart was filled with family. I needed to recharge for a big week of pop making.

# CHAPTER 13

*T*uesday

Maia splashed through the surface of the water in lane three, slid her goggles to her forehead, and checked the clock on the wall through the steam. The clock read 3:01.56. *Decent time!* she thought to herself. Maia took swim lessons after school every Tuesday at our future high school. Submerged underwater, it was a whole other world. She found peace in the quiet space while she stroked from wall to wall. It was an exhilarating change of environment from her otherwise busy, techy day-to-day life. This was where she got her best ideas and felt rejuvenated.

- *You try: Do you have a place you feel calm and*

*can recharge your positive attitude?*

She hopped out of the lane. "All done with the last my laps, Coach," she told her swim instructor, who was standing nearby.

"Nice work, Maia! We'll see you next week, and good job learning the butterfly stroke," her coach said, high-fiving her on the way to the locker room.

Maia knew it was her one long day each week. She had school and swim, then had to help her mom with her baby brother tonight. But she didn't mind. She loved it all.

On Tuesdays, she knew Maci and Mila would hold down the fort at Marshmallow Magic. They were busy making fifty pops tonight for the biggest-ever order, while Maia had swim and sibling duties.

Her mom was waiting outside the locker room holding nine-month-old Josh on her hip.

"Hi, sweetie!" her mom called out cheerfully. "You looked great out there!"

Josh was pulling at her hair while holding Stuffy—his favorite plush toy hippopotamus. It fell to the ground suddenly, and he winced. Maia ran to the rescue, delivering it to him with a tickle. Josh squirmed with delight and reached out for her.

Josh was Maia's half brother. They had the same mom, but Josh's dad was Maia's stepdad, Ben. He was a dentist during the day and super fun dad at night. He had met Maia's mom three years ago at a work conference a couple years after she and Maia's real dad had parted ways.

Maia was pretty young when these changes happened, so it felt like she had known her blended family most her life. She also had two stepsisters, Mei and Jun, who took care of her like a precious gemstone. They still played toys with her, asked her about her day, did lots of baking together, and gave her girl advice. They were at a basketball tournament tonight, so Maia's mom needed some extra help with Josh while she got some things done at the house.

Maia couldn't wait to get home and play with Josh. His favorite game was hide-and-seek, but she couldn't make it too hard. She hid behind obvious places like the couch or a corner until she heard the shuffle of his crawling nearing. Then, with delight, he'd peer around the corner and laugh until he tipped over in his puffy diaper.

While she kept an eye on him playing with a shape-sorting toy, Maia uploaded a couple of pictures of their recent order in progress to the Marshmallow Magic social media page on her laptop. She chose a close-up shot of one of the owls, with the rest of the owl flock blurred out in the background. She also uploaded a cute selfie of the three girls in aprons mid–pop dip. She wrote the caption: "Three wise friends making magic happen!"

And she knew they did have to make magic happen this week if their social reputation was going to shine.

*** 

Maci and I were jamming through the fifty pops back up in the fort. It takes us roughly two minutes a pop if we're efficient.

We made a combination of the owls and alphabet letter pops in various colors. We ended up choosing the cereal to make the letters. It was like breakfast meets dessert. We hoped the kids at Mrs. Bradley's events would like them.

*** 

Fast forward through one crazy week to Friday. We were getting really good at making owl and alphabet pops. We had it down to a system. By Friday, we had barely any mistake pops, which is a good thing because they waste money but kind of a sad thing since we usually get to eat them!

As I finished up the final pops, Maia and Maci began wrapping the rest individually in cellophane and sealing them with golden twist ties. They stuck a signature Marshmallow Magic sticker on top of every pop, which also had our website on it in case anyone wanted to learn more about our business. I made the customary thank-you card. I was feeling especially inspired after completing our big order.

We divided up the owls and alphabet pops evenly into four groups of fifty pops. We placed them neatly in boxes with display cups and ribbons and put them in the fort fridge, ready for the big delivery early tomorrow morning to the four libraries.

# CHAPTER 14

I awoke Saturday morning to Mrs. Bradley shaking my shoulders gently, asking, "Where are my pops? It's nine thirty, and you're late!"

I panicked and sprang upright, looking under my blankets and pillows for Mrs. Bradley's pops.

Oh. Oops.

Um, guess that was my mom waking me up. Not Mrs. Bradley.

Thankfully, Mom was waking me up to get ready to deliver the pops. I even had time for breakfast and teeth brushing. Possibly flossing. Phew!

OK, stress won't stop me. Breathe, Mila.

But *Biggest order ever!* rang inside my head, as if sprinkles were shaking every which way inside me.

"Biggest order ever!" my mom whispered, knowing how exciting this day was for me.

After breezing through my morning steps and a pile of pancakes, I met Maci and Maia up in the fort at 7:50 a.m.

"Biggest order ever!" we all squeaked, with slightly scratchy early-morning voices.

We carefully put the pop boxes, one at a time, into the basket and lowered them to the ground. Maci walked them to my mom's car. Once they were all loaded, we were off to deliver two hundred pops!

The first stop was our local library—the Westmont Library on Cobblestone Circle. I'd been here countless times, filling my arms up with exciting books about animals, science, art, sports, and more. This time, we were giving back.

There was a table set up near the front with Mrs. Bradley's Reading Adventures logo on various flyers and signs. We politely gave the pops to the man working that table and explained how to display them in the jars. He thanked us, and we were off to the next stop.

We dropped the pops off at the East Creekside Library about ten minutes away, then the Rock Point Library another fifteen minutes from that.

We finally arrived at the Twisted Creek Library: the fourth delivery location. It was 8:50 a.m., just in time for Mrs. Bradley's event to begin. The library was one of the smaller ones at the far end of the county. It was painted on the inside with bright murals of nature scenes with animals.

There were toddler-size tables in the far corner, stocked with baskets of crayons and paper for budding artists to keep busy. They had aisles of books that seemed to hold about half the amount we had at our library, but still many to choose from. Some books were displayed in bins, with their interesting covers facing outward for kids to see.

The librarians were busily working behind the checkout counter, ready for the doors to open to the line of residents waiting outside. One of them was talking with Mrs. Bradley in a warm, friendly voice. "We are just so grateful for your program. I know so many families that want to help their kids to read but aren't sure how. Having an exciting family reading event makes all the difference, especially for children with dyslexia."

Mrs. Bradley replied, "Well, it's our pleasure. You were saying there were a few families who contacted you personally whose children were really frustrated at school."

"Yes, sometimes having a fun library experience can be a breakthrough for the kids," the librarian continued.

I wasn't quite sure what they were talking about, but I hoped the Reading Adventures program would help.

Mrs. Bradley suddenly noticed that we had arrived and turned to us. She put up her hands with delight and said, "The pops are here!"

"Good morning, Mrs. Bradley!" we all said, excited to show her all our hard work.

Maci opened up the box to reveal a gorgeous fall-colored splendor of sweet treats. The pops were sparkling with sugar, lined up in neat rows.

"Oh, how adorable! They look so professional! The kids are just going to love them," Mrs. Bradley said. "Girls, you really do wonderful work. Thank you. Will you please set them up at the table over there?"

We all beamed with pride and went to set up the pops. As we did, families began entering the library and roaming around the aisles. Small children darted from their parents' knees and to the tables with crayons. Others took picture books to flip through and plopped down on cushy beanbag chairs.

I noticed Parker there with his dad. I wondered if his dad was asking him to check out some books since he had no reading points on Mrs. Driscoll's gemstone sticker chart. While his dad was trying to talk to him, Parker had the same glassy eyes he did at school. Just staring out somewhere—somewhere sad.

An Empathy Alert was kicking in full force. What was wrong with Parker?

"Guys, I'm worried about Parker. He's over there and has the same sad look he has at school," I said.

"He always seems happy at recess playing basketball," Maia said.

Maci shared, "He told me he's having trouble reading and is embarrassed to stay after school for help."

"I feel bad for him. But what could we do?" I said. "I'm sure the last thing he wants are some girls from school circling him when he's already uncomfortable."

We had just ignited joy across the library for so many kids with our festive pops, yet there seemed to be nothing we could do to help our good friend.

Maci, Maia, and I all just stood there. Blank looks on our faces. Helpless.

# CHAPTER 15

Suddenly drawing our attention away from Parker, Maci said, "Wow, there's a line of parents and kids coming in now," as she looked at what was now a very busy library.

Parents began eyeing the Reading Adventures table, and some took flyers to read about the program. It did two things: (1) hosted story time at the library, and (2) helped parents to find the right level books for their kids.

"Well, we have our first story time starting now in the reading nook over there," said Mrs. Bradley, pointing to a cozy side of the library covered in soft carpet near a large window bay.

Parents began to nestle into spots on the rug as one of the ladies working with Mrs. Bradley sat in a chair in the front. I nudged Maci as I saw Parker's dad try to pull his hand toward the rug. Parker's feet seemed stuck in cement. He wasn't moving.

Soon, the lady began, "Good morning, children and families! My name is Miss Karoline, and I'm with the wonderful Reading Adventures program. I'm doing our first story time this morning, and there will be one at promptly nine a.m. and three thirty p.m. this Monday and Wednesday." Miss Karoline seemed passionate about reading yet noticeably strict as she ordered silence on the rug, and pointed out the rule for no drinks inside the library.

More and more kids filled the empty spots on the rug as Karoline held up a large, beautiful book.

"*Under the Autumn Tree,*" Karoline announced as she showed the cover of the selected book to the audience. She began reading with such rich passion, turning each page with excitement. She involved the children occasionally, asking questions to the audience. Children wildly raised their hands, hoping to be chosen to share their ideas.

Parents hugged their kids as the book ended with a happy twist. Parker, on the other hand, hugged his knees. He was still in the far corner of the library but now on the floor.

Then, Karoline invited children to wander the library

and find a book (with a reminder to walk, not run), then visit the Reading Adventures table to pick a second book that the program recommended. Kids grabbed a marshmallow pop and their books, then bounced off to cozy spots to read with their parents.

Then suddenly, we felt it happening. Something that happened during every Marshmallow Magic event when kids began eating the pops.

Our super Smart Senses ignited—kind of like a sugar rush.

- *Smart Senses: You may have heard of IQ—something that measures how smart you are about solving problems. Remember, Smart Senses are how much you know about emotions. It's when you know how you feel and can see, hear, and guess what others may be feeling. "Empathy" means guessing how others are feeling.*

Maia is great at *watching* how people act to guess how they're feeling. Maci *listens* to what people say to understand how they feel. Me? Well, I *read minds*. I can figure out what people are probably thinking and feeling. I notice all the factors and figure out why they may be sad, happy, lonely, frustrated, mad, or any other emotion.

"Empathy Alert, guys," Maia said solemnly, gesturing over to the carpet area. She had noticed one boy who stayed on the rug. His shiny black hair hung over his face, which appeared worried as he peeked out. His body was curled up, with his shoulders slouched down. His mom was talking to him in a loving voice, pointing at the shelves of books. As she tried to pull him up, he seemed glued to the rug.

Maci commented, "Did you hear that? His mom just said, 'You loved story time, Kaden; why not look at the other wonderful books here?' But he said back, 'I hate reading, Mom! Can we go home now?' How sad."

"He seems to feel left out. Nervous about something. He instantly changed from happy and interested in the book Karoline was reading to sad when it was his turn to read. Hmm, I wonder if we can help," I chimed in.

I grabbed a marshmallow pop and a book on dinosaurs from the early reader section and slowly walked over to Kaden.

# CHAPTER 16

I reached the pop out to Kaden, eyeing his mom for permission. She nodded with a warm smile.

"Hey, buddy," I said. "I'm dying to see if this stegosaurus on the cover of this book finds his family. Would you like to join me to snack on this pop while we check out the story?"

Kaden shyly peered at his mom, then at the toy dinosaur figure he was holding that had been my clue to snag this particular book, then back at me. He nodded, and I led him over to some beanbag chairs by the mural.

He started to perk up a little with the marshmallow pop as I read the first couple of pages.

"Do you want to read this page about the dinosaur crossing the river?" I asked.

Kaden shook his head no.

I could tell he was nervous about his reading skills, but I also wanted him to try to learn.

"Well, maybe you could help me with this word. I've never seen it before, and it looks like an important word," I said, pointing to the word *Roar!!!* that was written in big letters.

"Rrrr," Kaden murmured.

"Yes, that sounds right! What sound do the *o* and *a* make together?" I continued.

"Ooooo," Kaden replied.

"And the *r*?" I asked.

"Rrrr," Kaden said slightly louder.

"Great, Kaden!" I said. "Now can you put them all together?"

"Rrrraaoo," he said, stammering through the word.

Realizing he still had some learning to do, I wanted him to be encouraged. "Great try! Roar is the word," I said, hoping to keep his attention. I went ahead and finished reading the book, asking for Kaden to sound out a word on each page.

"What an exciting book! It was so much fun reading with you, Kaden. Would you like to check out the book?" I asked.

"OK," he said. His mom was beaming with a happy tear in her eye.

Meanwhile, I couldn't help but notice that Parker, in the other corner of the library, also had a tear in his eye.

***

Maci, Maia, and I stayed a little longer, watching the marshmallow pops disappear as quickly as the flyers. Mrs. Bradley was fluttering around, talking to the parents and kids. She came over to us and said, "Girls, not only did you do a fantastic job on the pops, but they helped get all the kids to the table to find a book on their level! Here is the payment for the pops."

I took the envelope from Mrs. Bradley and thanked her.

"Maci, Maia...Mrs. Bradley said the pops helped get all the kids to the table to find a book. I can't stop thinking about it. Not *all* the kids went over. There were a few kids, like Kaden and Parker, that didn't want to check out books," I said.

"You're right. I wonder if they have trouble reading," Maci said.

"But how can we help? We're not teachers," Maia added.

Just then one of the librarians came up to us.

"Hi, girls! What wonderful pops you made for the event today! Which one of you is Mila?" she asked.

I raised my hand quickly.

"Mila, I heard about the great job you did with Kaden. His mother was grateful for your help inspiring him to read," she continued.

"Oh, it was nothing. I didn't feel like I helped much—we just sounded out a few letters," I said.

"Well, his mom said that is the first time he tried reading letters and words out loud since school began," she explained. "Kaden has dyslexia, which makes it hard for him to read correctly. You built up his confidence and inspired him to check out his first book!"

"Wow, I had no idea. Happy I could help! Is dyslexia common?" I asked.

"It is, and every child who has it learns uniquely. It doesn't mean they're not smart; their brain just sees the words in ways that may be different than other readers," the librarian elaborated.

"That would be hard. Glad I could encourage him. I definitely have felt left out before."

We said goodbye and checked out a few books ourselves (well, Maci lugged out like a gazillion books) and went back to the tree fort.

***

I walked in the fort and sat down on the edge of the twill couch.

"Something just doesn't feel right," I said. "Something has to change. Something big."

I opened up the envelope from Mrs. Bradley. It read, "$400.00." I stared at it thoughtfully. Then suddenly, I knew what I had to do.

Maia and Maci looked stunned as I slapped Mrs. Bradley's check on the table.

"We're not keeping this money," I said with certainty.

# CHAPTER 17

The check lay on the table. It was strangely quiet as we all stared at the large dollar amount.

After digging deep into what I was feeling, I said, "This is the biggest check we've ever received. We can do anything with the money. Buy larger, better pop stands. Make new glossy marketing flyers. Hire a photographer to do a pop photo shoot.

"But we're doing well as a business. Really well. Our cake pop sales are great, and we have plenty of supplies. And even if we didn't, the point is to make people happy. Remember when we began Marshmallow Magic? We were looking for a way to have fun baking. We wanted to make people smile and help make great parties.

"We spend all this time making treats to make people happy.

Sure, our pops helped kids get interested in reading, but there are probably many kids like Kaden and Parker who feel inferior. Kids who need help reading."

Maci chimed in, "Yeah, kids like Kaden may feel like they're not as smart as other kids. They may feel really left out at Mrs. Bradley's reading events."

"Like how I feel when it's cake time at birthday parties," I added quietly.

Maci and Maia suddenly jumped to my side with a couple of sugar-sweet hugs.

I love my friends!

Maci continued, "What if there are more kids like Kaden that no one noticed?"

"Wow, about ten percent of people may have dyslexia," Maia said, referencing the quick search she did on the tree fort computer.

With all of us feeling a bit deflated at how we could possibly help so many kids learn to read, Maia finally broke the silence that had grown in the tree house. "Don't forget how much you helped Kaden by just being positive, Mila," she said.

"That's true," Maci agreed. "Kaden didn't want to read with his mom but seemed open to reading with a kid."

"But I'm just one kid. I can't help everyone," I said.

As I searched my mind for an answer, my thoughts began to drift. I gazed around the tree fort. Wicker baskets neatly lined shelves from the ceiling to the floor. Metal tags with chalkboard plates on them revealed the contents inside, like "Candy melts," "Cellophane wrappers," and "Pop sticks."

White packaging boxes were stacked in a cubby. Photos of happy customers with their pops were strung along a wire above the fridge and sink.

Trays full of colored paper, cardstock, and stationery were organized on the table.

A robot vacuum was docked in a corner, awaiting action on any stray sprinkle.

Everywhere I looked, money had paid for an abundance of supplies and tools.

I thought back to when the idea for Marshmallow Magic had begun. It was Valentine's Day of kindergarten. I was making lovey-dovey trail mix in the kitchen with my mom. It had cereal, candy hearts, pretzel sticks, chocolate chips, and mini marshmallows. I was playing with the mix and had the idea to put a pretzel stick into a marshmallow and dip it into melted chocolate chips. My brother spilled sprinkles on them, and Marshmallow Magic was born! The kitchen was a wreck, but we were so happy to create treats. We sold them at a table in our driveway to many happy neighbors and made eleven dollars!

We had almost no fancy supplies, yet we had all we needed.

We had to do more with the money we made.

Maia was still browsing on her computer when a notification popped up on social media with a post from her sister Jun. It showed a slo-mo video of her sinking a three-pointer, with the caption, "Nothing but net!" followed by the hashtag #collegebound.

"Hold the sprinkles, girls! I've got it!" she suddenly exclaimed, her face illuminated by both the computer screen and a newfound smile. "I know exactly how we can help."

# CHAPTER 18

O K. Maia's idea was spectacular. Fireworks spectacular. The idea let us use our money to help countless kids.

It was brilliant, but we needed to take action immediately, before the library events ended. And we had a stop to make first.

Maci, Maia, and I felt Marshmallow Magic magic like never before. We quickly slid one after another down the tree fort pole.

"Charge!" we all yelled as we hopped on our bikes off to save the world—well, at least, it felt like it.

We made our first stop at Maia's house. We found her sister Jun easily. She was still in the driveway shooting hoops like we'd seen in her video post. We shared our big idea with her, and she was all in.

We all biked over to the Twisted Creek Library to put the plan in action.

*** 

I looked around the library, noticing more than ever the different expressions on kids as they read. One young girl had her dark-brown hair woven into two braids alongside her very animated face. She was reading in a high-pitched voice, imitating some character in the brightly colored picture book she clutched tightly.

A boy at the table next to her appeared a bit more serious. His blue eyes were wide open, peering at the pages of a much thicker book. He read aloud in a low, steady voice, carefully pronouncing each word.

Another girl lay on her back, book propped up in the air above her head to read. Her legs wiggled back and forth with excitement, perhaps to mirror each twist in the plot of her storybook.

A boy on the far side of the library stared out a window at a cluster of squirrels racing around a tree. A stack of books sat untouched alongside him.

An older teen sat with headphones, papers spread out across a long table in the back. He was engrossed in textbooks, unruffled by the toddlers who scrambled by on the way to the picture book section.

The library was truly a **myriad** of young learners of every age, reading level, and book interests. Suddenly, I felt a surge of honor about the chance to help such a wide range of kids.

- *myriad: mix or assortment of things*
- *You try: The box of _____ I gave my mom had a myriad of flavors to try.*

I pulled Maci and Maia by the hands into a small huddle and said, "Ready? Now is the time! Look around at all the readers we can help. Some need help reading, some need inspiration, and some just need a friend."

\*\*\*

We introduced Jun to Parker and his dad. Jun had brought a book on Michael Jordan, arguably the best basketball player that ever lived. After a short chat, Parker seemed interested in checking out the book with Jun, and they were off to a brightly lit book nook.

Our plan was working!

We next needed to find Mrs. Bradley.

After spotting her behind the checkout counter, I looked at Maci and Maia and said, "Are we sure about this?"

"One hundred percent!" they replied, and I pulled out our Marshmallow Magic checkbook. Maia smiled and pulled out a peacock-feathered pen. Maci did a silent cheer, and we knew we were all in.

I wrote Mrs. Bradley's business name, "Reading Adventures," on the "To" line and wrote "$200.00" in the dollar amount box.

We all walked over to Mrs. Bradley, trying hard to contain our excitement to help her business with our donation.

"Hi, Mrs. Bradley. We have an idea about how to help more kids to read, while helping older kids headed to college," I said.

"Oh, I'd love to hear what you have in mind," she replied.

We then went on to describe how:

- Little kids look up to high school kids and love reading with them
- High school kids want ways to make money
  - Helping the community is a great thing for high

school kids to put on their college applications

And our idea:

- Use our $200 to pay high school kids to read with little kids
- Match the kids by common interest (like Jun and Parker liking basketball) to bond better

"So, little kids get help reading with someone they look up to, while high school kids get money and experience for college," Mrs. Bradley said, charged with emotion.

"Please accept our donation to help," I said proudly, handing over the check.

I wasn't sure if Mrs. Bradley looked like she was about to cheer or cry. She stood there for a while, clutching the check. She looked at each of us with such intensity, yet no words.

Finally, through a shaky voice, she spoke, "Girls, I'm so impressed with you. I am so grateful for this kind donation. You've not only brought attention to the Reading Adventures program with your pops, but through your amazing empathy for these readers, you found a way to help kids with dyslexia by finding them a reading buddy they look up to. Your ability to notice what people are feeling and need is amazing."

We were all beaming with hope and happiness for the families in our neighborhood.

"Girls, you are an inspiration to our community," Mrs. Bradley said. "I love the idea, and I think we need to rename this reading program! I'm thinking *Magic Book Buddies* has a nice ring to it."

The buddies idea was really working. Parker continued to sit with Jun as he read with confidence about basketball, his eyes now unglazed and focused on the story of the superstar athlete.

We sat down with Mrs. Bradley and made a plan to have high schoolers sign up for the Magic Book Buddies program, listing their hobbies and activities. We wanted to match up every single kid in the reading program with a high schooler that had something in common. Whether it was baking, skateboarding, dragons, or skiing, everyone would have a match.

"Where are they?" I asked Maia, unsure if I was whispering in a library voice or sneaky voice. Maia smiled and slowly revealed three extra owl pops we'd hidden in a small cooler for us. We all tore open the packages, proud to celebrate all the problems we solved for the biggest order ever.

I really felt a part of this tasty celebration, not left out as I often do. In fact, my food allergies didn't seem like a big deal at all right now. I felt empowered, kind and free, all at the same time—maybe like the blue jay.

And just as thoughts of that bird filled my head, Maci suddenly said, "Look!" pointing to the blue jay sitting just outside the window by Parker in his reading nook. "Is that the same bird that came to the tree house with the candy corn?"

"Looks like it!" Maia said.

Well, magic certainly was everywhere. Maybe somehow, someway, this blue jay had something to do with it.

What I did know is that Maci, Maia, and I had a *lot* to do with it, and it felt great.

# Cool New Words

- **concoction:** *a mixture of various ingredients*
- *You try: My friend and I used a concoction of_____ and _____to make _____.*

- **intercept:** *to stop something or keep something from happening*
- *You try: I intercepted my dad at the front door before he could see the _____ I had made for his birthday.*

- **verify:** *to make sure*
- *You try: I had to verify that my parents said I could _____, because they normally say it's too dangerous.*

- **unruly:** *wild, disorderly*
- *You try: Our new puppy was so unruly as he _____in our living room.*

- **inferior**: *worse than something else*
- *You try: The _____my brother made were inferior to the ones my mom makes.*

- **unison**: *at the same time*
- *You try: On Christmas morning, me and my little brother ran down the stairs in unison to _____.*

- **sprawling:** *spread out over a large area*
- *You try: My sprawling _____ were on my messy bedroom floor.*

- **notion:** *idea*
- *You try: I didn't like the notion of getting up at _____ a.m.*

- **perimeter:** *all the sides of a shape added up*

- **invigorate:** *to make full of energy and excitement*
- *You try: Invigorated by the warm air, I went to the park and _____.*

- **desolate:** *empty and quiet; no signs of life*
- *You try: The playground seemed desolate because the weather was so _____.*

- **serenely:** *calmly*
- *You try: After studying all weekend for the spelling test, I serenely_____.*

- **pulley system**: *A rope wrapped around a wheel. The rope is attached to something heavy, and when the wheel turns, it pulls that object to a new place.*

- **sporadic:** *every now and then*
- *You try: My sporadic attendance at basketball practice meant that _____.*

- **embellishment**: *decoration*
- *You try: I wanted my _____ for my grandma to be extra special, so I glued on embellishments before I put it in the envelope.*

- **nocturnal**: *awake during the night, asleep during the day*
- *You try: I really think my teenage brother is nocturnal because he_____.*

- **pierogi:** *a Polish food similar to a dumpling filled with cheese, potatoes, or other fillings*

- **myriad:** *mix or assortment of things*
- *You try: The box of _____ I gave my mom had a myriad of flavors to try.*

# Smart Senses

OK. Being school smart is important. Sure, we all know that. But did you know what else is super-duper important? How you feel! If you can understand how you and others feel, you're going to have a way better life. That doesn't mean you'll always be happy. Being sad, scared, or mad are totally normal. It's how you choose to act that matters.

I learned an awesome trick called Smart Senses to help. These are a bunch of cool ways to tune in to how you're feeling so you can decide what to do. Ready?

- **Smart Sense #1: Positive Peepers** – Fake glasses that help you focus on the positive things in life, even though sad stuff is there too.

- You try: Can you think of a time something sad happened but you saw the good side?

- **Smart Sense #2: Body Bonkers** – When your body goes crazy before you realize you're worried about something. Like a woozy tummy, a headache, or jittery thoughts that keep coming like a waterfall.

- You try: What are some crazy things your body does when you're worried?

- **Smart Sense #3: Empathy Alert** – *When you use clues to figure out how someone is feeling.*
- *You try: When the girls had an Empathy Alert for Parker, what did they think he was feeling? Why?*

- **Smart Sense #4: Wild Worry** – *When you can't stop worrying about something and think about all the bad things that could happen.*
- *You try: What are the top three things you worry about?*

- **Smart Sense #5: Brain Brakes** – *Something you do that stops you from worrying. Playing sports or seeing facts helps Maci calm down.*
- *You try: What helps you calm down? Do you have a place you feel calm and can recharge your positive attitude?*

- *effervescence: bubbles in a liquid; enthusiasm*
- *You try: Do you have friends that make you laugh or help you stay positive like effervescence?*

### What Is a Food Allergy?

*A food allergy is when my body thinks a food is bad. If I eat it, my body tries to keep me safe by tightening my blood vessels. My face, mouth, and chest also could get itchy and rashy. My throat could swell, making it harder for me to breathe, which is why it's really important I stay away from these foods. I wish I could just tell my body, "Hey, a peanut butter cup is a good thing." But that's nature for you. And I can't change it. --Mila*

# Author Biography

Gail Gilla Czyszczon has been a writing professional for more than two decades in a variety of settings, including Z3 Writing, her copywriting business. She holds a master's degree in family therapy from the University of San Diego. As a mother to a daughter with food allergies, the nexus of her profession and passion lies in raising awareness among young readers on food allergies and social-emotional skills. The Marshmallow Magic book series is inspired by a marshmallow and cake pop business her daughter began in first grade.

Czyszczon grew up in Chicago and currently lives in San Diego with her husband and two children. When she's not writing, she enjoys running, skiing, boating, and playing cards.

Learn more about her books at www.marshmallowmagic.com or visit facebook.com/marshmallowmagicbooks.com.